Goldie the Dollmaker

Goldie the Dollmaker

M. B. Goffstein

Farrar · Straus · Giroux

New York

To my brother, Bob

Goldie the Dollmaker

Goldie Rosenzweig's parents were dead so she lived alone in their house and went on with her father's work of carving small wooden dolls, and her mother's work of painting bright clothes and friendly faces on them. In four years she had carved, painted, and sold as many dolls as her parents used to do in eight, and there were always more orders for her dolls than she could fill.

Goldie Rosenzweig fought hard and quietly to get a new doll's face free from the bit of wood that was smothering it, and once she had carved the head and body she could not lay it down on the worktable and go to bed. She felt responsible for the little wooden person who would not exist but for her, so she went through the wood basket until she found four sticks of wood that really looked as if they wanted to make arms and legs for the new doll.

She laid them on the table and tucked the doll into her pocket while she made herself some dinner. Then

Goldie stayed up all night, measuring and carving a little pair of arms with hands and a little pair of legs with shoes on their feet.

When she put the doll together with pins that would allow its arms and legs to be moved, the sun was shining and Goldie went to bed. Her own joints felt much stiffer than the doll's.

Goldie woke up at noon and thought of the new doll at once. She got right out of bed and sat down at the worktable and looked at the doll for a long time.

Then she reached for her knife and sat in her nightgown until late afternoon, absorbed in the careful work of making the new doll as nice to look at and as agreeable and cozy to hold as possible. She ate a bun and drank some tea, washed up, and got back to work.

At dusk the little doll was done. Then Goldie swept and cleaned, and when everything was good she washed herself and brushed her hair back, put on a clean nightgown, and sat down by the door. She folded her hands in her lap and thought about the carpenter who made the wooden crates for her dolls.

Omus Hirschbein was handsome and friendly and exactly her age, but it was because he made things out of wood that Goldie often thought about him. She felt that they were alike and should be good friends.

The next morning Goldie got out her paints and carefully mixed a flesh color for the doll. She covered its face, neck, and ears, its arms and hands with the rosy tan paint, and then waited for it to dry.

As the day went on, Goldie ate buns and drank tea, and painted the doll's curls a glossy dark brown. She painted a white camisole and matching knickers on the doll's body, gray stockings on her legs and pretty black shoes on her feet. Then she painted a little gleaming black eye on either side of the doll's nose and finally, holding it firmly around the waist with one hand, Goldie smiled and smiled into the doll's eyes in the friendliest, sweetest way, and she painted a smile right back to herself on the little doll's face.

That smile was why shops could not keep Goldie Rosenzweig's dolls in stock, and that smile was why there were more orders for her dolls than she could

fill. There was no little girl, no parent, aunt, or uncle of a little girl anywhere in the world who could see a little wooden doll that smiled with such friendliness and sweetness, and then buy a different doll to take home. They said that if you looked at a Goldie Rosenzweig doll you bought her, even if you weren't going to buy any doll in the first place. Because the truth about that smile was that it was heartbreaking.

It was the most satisfying thing to hold a little Goldie Rosenzweig doll in your hand and know that she was going to be kissed a lot and taken everywhere, be given the best doll's wardrobe in the world, and made very happy.

One day three little wooden dolls sat facing each other for company on the worktable because Goldie Rosenzweig was going out. She pulled on her boots, got into her jacket, and tied a kerchief under her chin. "I am going to get your crate," she said, "and I won't be gone long."

Then she went out the door of her parents' house, walked quickly across a field and slowly through a little forest, where she had the good luck to find enough wood for two more dolls before she came to the carpenter's shop.

"Hello, Goldie," said Omus Hirschbein, "what can I do for you today?"

"I've made three more dolls and I need another crate."

"That's fine," said Omus. "I can have one ready for you in an hour."

"Oh, thank you! And could you keep this wood for me while I go shopping?"

"Sure, Goldie, but I'd still like to know why you don't ever want to use my wood scraps."

Goldie shook her head. "I just don't like to use pieces of wood that are all clean and square from the saw."

"But your parents always did. It saved them a lot of trouble."

"I remember," said Goldie. "I don't see how they could."

"But what difference does it make?"

"It just doesn't seem as real, so it's not as interesting to carve. And then it doesn't turn out as good. It never looks alive."

Omus pushed back his cap and scratched his head. "They're just dolls, Goldie."

"I know, but I make them. So to me they're not just dolls. I have to love making them. And besides, to little girls they're not just dolls—"

"All right, all right!" Omus laughed. "I believe
you!"

He took Goldie's wood into his shop and she walked on, until she came to the town.

The sun was shining on the dancing treetops above the dappled shady street and Goldie walked along excitedly, looking into all the shops.

In the dim, dusty hardware store she bought a pound of nails and a pot of blue paint from old Mr. Gottesman, who rubbed his plump hands together briskly and beamed at her through his glasses. "Well, well, well," he said. "You do a good business,

so I do a good business! Your poor parents never did such a business."

"I don't think they cared about it as much as I do," said Goldie. "Didn't the little pins I ordered come in yet?"

"Of course not!" cried Mr. Gottesman. "That was a special order, and a special order takes time."

"Well, I'll come in again next week," she said, and went out the door and on down the street.

"Goldie!" Mrs. Stern called from her bakery. "I'll

bet you smelled the buns I just took out of the oven."

"Mm–m–m." Goldie came into the shop and sniffed the delicious warm smell. "I certainly do now!" And Mrs. Stern chuckled delightedly.

Just then a little girl walked in, holding a Goldie Rosenzweig doll in her hand. "You can choose anything you want," she was telling it earnestly, "anything at all."

"Rosie," said Mrs. Stern, and she winked at Goldie. "Do you know who—"

"No!" whispered Goldie, shaking her head at Mrs.

Stern. Then she stood shyly and proudly, watching the little girl Rosie and her doll until they chose a big round sugar cookie and went out trading bites.

"Wasn't that sweet!" said Mrs. Stern.

Goldie nodded happily. "I just don't like to say that I make the dolls," she apologized. "It just doesn't seem right." She bought a dozen buns and said goodbye to Mrs. Stern. Then she went across the street to her favorite store.

Mr. Solomon imported beautiful things from all

over the world, and he sold as many of Goldie Rosenzweig's dolls as he could get. He rose as she came into his gloomy, fragrant shop. "Well, Goldie, have you brought me any dolls today?"

"No, but I will next week," she promised. "I just came in now to buy some tea."

"I've got a new kind that I think you will like," he said, but Goldie didn't hear him. An exquisite little lamp had caught her eye, and she was kneeling in front of the low table it stood on.

"Ah," said Mr. Solomon. "That little Chinese lamp."

"Oh-h, it's lovely," breathed Goldie, stroking the fragile porcelain globe with her finger.

"You have good taste." Mr. Solomon smiled and his gold tooth shone. "I'm glad you could see it before I sent it away."

"Why? Has someone bought it? Has it been sold?" Goldie's throat ached.

"Who would buy it?" he asked. "It is such a small thing for so much money. No one would buy it."

Goldie touched the gleaming china base, examined the little carved wooden stand, and looked up at Mr.

Solomon. "So I am sending it to my brother's store," he continued. "He has wealthy customers who appreciate good things." And shaking his head sadly over his own customers, Mr. Solomon went to the back of the store to measure out the tea.

Goldie stayed with the little lamp. "Mr. Solomon," she said, when he came back with her tea, "if I sold twenty-seven of my dolls, I could buy it."

"You want to buy this little lamp?"

"It's the most beautiful thing I've ever seen," she said.

"Well," said Mr. Solomon. "Well, just let me think for a minute."

Goldie stood up and looked around the store without much interest, while Mr. Solomon tapped his gold tooth with a pencil.

"Miss Rosenzweig," he said at last, "since you and I do business together, I can give you a special price on the lamp."

"Oh, thank you very much!"

Mr. Solomon held up his hand for silence. "Also," he said, "you save me the trouble of sending it to my brother. And," he pointed at the lamp, "you appreciate it."

"Oh, yes!"

"So I'll take off one third of the price for you, and you can take it home with you now."

"But it will take me three months to make eighteen dolls," said Goldie.

"Of course," said Mr. Solomon. "Meanwhile you can enjoy the lamp." He went to find the wooden crate it had come in, and Goldie took out her money to pay for the tea.

But when he came back, Mr. Solomon waved it away. "The tea is a present," he said. "It's not every day I make such a big sale."

It was already growing dark when, holding the precious crate, Goldie walked carefully through the fallen leaves, back to Omus Hirschbein's shop.

"What have you got there?" he asked her, looking curiously at the Chinese writing on the top of the crate.

"You aren't going to start having your doll crates made in China, are you?"

"Oh no," Goldie laughed. "I bought something that came from China." She went inside the shop and carefully set it down. "I'll show you what it is," she said, and she lifted the little lamp out of its crate and stood it up on the counter. "Look. Isn't this beautiful?"

"It's cute," said Omus, "but it won't give you much light."

"No, really look at it! See how beautifully it's made and painted."

Omus looked more closely, and he saw the price tag. "Is that what you paid for it?" he asked in a voice filled with horror.

"I am paying one third less," said Goldie, "and I'm paying for it in dolls. But I would have paid the full price—I would have paid more! It's the most beautiful thing I've ever seen in my life."

"You know, Goldie," Omus said slowly, "I think you must be a real artist."

Goldie flushed with pleasure. "Why?" she asked him. "Why do you think so?"

"Because you're crazy."

"Oh." Goldie tried to smile.

"Here's your doll crate," said Omus, "and I'll put your wood and these little packages inside it so you'll have less to carry."

"Thank you."

Goldie laid the little lamp back in its crate but all her pleasure in it was gone, and as she walked back to her parents' house in the darkness, through the little forest and over the field, she was planning desperately to return it to Mr. Solomon early the next morning.

She was crazy to have bought it, no matter how beautiful it was. It *wouldn't* give much light, and it had cost so much that she would scarcely be able to eat for three months, until she had paid for it. And she would need more paint, and the little pins to attach the dolls' arms and legs with, and more crates . . .

And Goldie came home at last, feeling scared and sick and lonely. She wandered around inside the dark little house like a stranger, not wanting to sit in any of the chairs or lie down on the bed. And she tried not to look at the wooden crate with the Chinese writing on it, lying beside the three little wooden dolls on the worktable in the moonlight.

She felt empty inside, as if she were hollow, but the hollowness ached and pounded and finally, in a daze, she sat down by the door.

She stayed there for a long time, then she heard herself whisper, "I'm lonely."

"I'm so lonely," she said. Then she cried wearily until at last she fell asleep at her little place by the door.

She dreamed she felt a light tap on her shoulder.

"Please," said a warm, polite voice. "Please!"

"Yes?" said Goldie.

"That lamp you bought."

"Yes?"

"I made it."

"Oh, it's beautiful!" said Goldie.

"So we are friends."

"But I don't know you," she said. "I wish I did."

"You do know me," laughed the voice. "You know me better than the people I see every day."

"But who are you?"

"I made that lamp you bought today!"

"Oh," said Goldie. "Oh! I see." And she sat for a moment, smiling. "But you don't know me," she said suddenly.

"Yes I do. I made the lamp for you—whoever you are."

Goldie laughed and laughed.

"You understand!" cried the voice.

"Yes," said Goldie. "That's the way *I* carve little wooden dolls and paint their clothes and faces on them."

In the middle of the night, Goldie woke up. She went over to the worktable, lifted the little lamp out of its crate, and set it gently down and lighted it. Then she sat down and examined the scene that was painted on the globe.

A Chinese family was having a picnic by a little stream, beneath a lovely drooping tree. Two children were sailing flowers in the stream while an old man and woman in flowing robes sat on red chairs, watching. Three beautiful ladies knelt on the ground, preparing the dishes of food with slender, dainty fingers, and behind them, on a terrace, a gentle, beautiful man stood smiling. Each lovely line was alive with truth, and the deep, rich colors glowed.

The china base of the lamp was completely different. Wild black and white horses galloped and bucked and reared all around it, but their tails and manes made a calm, swirling design. And the black wooden base with its three round feet was simply carved to hold the lamp firmly in place.

Goldie let out her breath with a sigh of pleasure, and looked around the room.

After all, it was such a tiny house. The little lamp filled it all with a soft, cozy light.

"My house," Goldie thought for the first time in her life. "My own little house, with my knife and lamp and tea, my bed and worktable and wood, where I make little wooden dolls for friends."